The Wise Steward Book

for Children Only!

Stewardship Principles
in Biblical Creation

Written and Illustrated by Denise I. Griggs

Glass Tree Books®
Sacramento, CA

The Wise Steward Book

for Children Only!

Stewardship Principles
In Biblical Creation

Glass Tree Books®
P.O. Box 278475
Sacramento, CA 95827
www.glasstreebooks.com

Denise I. Griggs © 2020
ISBN: 978-0-615-24619-2
Library of Congress Control Number: 2020925945

Illustrations by Denise I. Griggs

Scriptural References from The Holy Bible, King James Version,
Thomas Nelson Inc., © 1972

Published by Glass Tree Books®
Sacramento, CA

To my Parents with Love

"You can't be successful while trying to drag somebody with you!"
…Mom

Special Thanks and Dedication

All love and glory to God for choosing me to research and author this book. Also, to my family for their love and support to whom I dedicate it. Special thanks to numerous others who encouraged me over the years to complete this project. Much appreciation!

PREFACE

The Wise Steward Book, for Children Only! is based on the Christian Bible and recognizes that God is the Creator and Owner of all.

In this book, Creation is the foundation and source for instruction in stewardship principles. We see that on each day of Creation, there are principles to prepare us for all life phases, from birth to death. These principles are an intentional pattern to imitate and live successful lives.

Understanding Creation stewardship principles will also help manage the "quality" of life. In our lifetimes and throughout history, we can see that good stewardship brings success, while poor stewardship brings disaster. Both good and bad stewardship affects everyone, even to future generations!

Knowing how to be a wise steward is a gift from God. The Bible states that we are to ask God for wisdom, and He will give it to us abundantly. *(James 1:5)* One Biblical example is when young Solomon became king; he prayed to God for the wisdom to be a good leader (steward) over the people in the kingdom entrusted to his care. He didn't pray for riches and honor, but because Solomon was honest and sincere, God not only gave him superior wisdom, but He also blessed Solomon with riches and honor. Solomon is known as the wisest and richest king in the Bible. *(II Chronicles 1:9-12)*

When someone, including God, entrusts us to take care of something that belongs to them, we are to manage it and care for it as if it were our own. We are to be dependable, trustworthy, and reliable stewards no matter the circumstances or conditions of our birth, race, culture, or country.

This book isn't to replace learning mathematics or accounting. It is to help understand the spiritual skills to use it properly. We need only to look around at all Creation and remember its stewardship principles and understand why God expects good stewardship from you and me!

INTRODUCTION

In the Bible, there is a story about a man named Nehemiah, a king's servant, who was incredibly sad when he heard that the wall and gates in his hometown were in disrepair. The people weren't safe from their enemies, and he was afraid that they would enter the town and destroy them. *(Nehemiah 1-6)*

To help solve the problem, the king gave Nehemiah permission to return home and help his people repair and rebuild. Once there, secretly, Nehemiah took a few men with him to survey the damage and devise a plan. Next, Nehemiah gathered his people and advised them that they could repair the damage by working together. They agreed, and while some stood guard, the rest worked day and night repairing the wall and gates. Parents brought their children, boys, and girls, to work alongside them to understand what it meant to build, repair, and improve.

While Nehemiah and his people worked, their enemies threatened them, but they wouldn't stop working. After only 52 days, they completed building the wall and gates. The people were secure again.

Everyone needs to plan, build, and repair the walls and security in their lives, especially with money. Although security is not just limited to money, one's financial health affects all relationships. How well someone manages their money decides the quality of life for oneself, their home, family, and communities.

For some people, creating a financial plan or rebuilding their finances might take only 52 days, just like the story of Nehemiah, or it might take all 52 weeks of the year. For some, it will take longer, but anyone can do it.

Children also need to participate and understand how to plan, build, budget, and repair the family finances. The Wise Steward Book, for Children Only! is just for that purpose!

DAYS OF CREATION FOR WISE STEWARDSHIP

Creation is an orderly progression of God's wise principles. By examining each created day, we can see the stewardship principles' pattern for the six days of Creation and the seventh day of rest listed below. A chart is on the next page.

Day:

1. Light
2. Firmament/Heaven
3. Seas, Earth, Vegetation, Seeds
4. Sun, Moon, and Stars
5. Fish and Birds
6. Animals and Mankind
7. Rest - *Creation was in six days, but the 7th day is equally important*

Principles of Each Day:

1. Giving First
2. Obedience to Authority
3. Continuity
4. Preparation
5. Provision
6. Unconditional Love
7. Balance

Wise Stewardship Actions:

1. Tithes
2. Taxes
3. Offerings
4. Savings
5. Family
6. Sharing
7. Surplus

CREATION CHART FOR WISE STEWARDSHIP

DAY	CREATION	STEWARD PRINCIPLE	ACTION	VISUAL EXAMPLE	BIBLE VERSE
1	Light	Giving First	Tithes		*Malachi 3:10*
2	Firmament, or Heaven	Obedience to Authority	Taxes		*Luke 20:25*
3	Seas, Earth, Vegetation, Seeds	Continuity	Offerings		*II Corin. 9:7*
4	Sun, Moon, and Stars	Preparation	Savings		*Matthew 25:20*
5	Fish and Birds	Provision	Family		*I Timothy 5:8*
6	Animals, and Man	Unconditional Love	Sharing		*Luke 6:38*
7	Rest	Balance	Surplus		*Proverbs 10:22*

STEWARDSHIP

What is a steward or stewardship, and what does it have to do with managing assets, especially money? Why does anyone need to know it? Most dictionaries explain that stewards are:

- Someone who manages their own money
- Someone hired to manage the affairs of a person, or business owner
- A Bookkeeper or Accountant who maintain accounts for others

Wise owners will clearly instruct their stewards of the goals they have for their assets, which can be the stewardship of their home, business, finances, and children. Likewise, wise stewards will follow the owner's instructions.

Wise owners will consistently review their assets and the steward's management of them and make timely changes with their money or stewards if necessary. A wise owner gives their stewards regular and timely progress reports. Thankfully, anyone can review their stewardship as often as needed and make the appropriate corrections.

More importantly, a wise owner and wise steward must know and understand both spiritual and natural stewardship management skills, then combine them in their management duties. Therefore they must incorporate:

1) The Bible (reading all of it)
2) Basic Life and Relationships Skills
3) Reading, Comprehension, and Mathematics
4) Budgets for both Time and Money

With God as our Source, Owner, Wise Steward, and Guide, He will never ask us to do anything too hard or impossible for us to do, nor will He ever expect us to do anything that He hasn't already done for us. How do we know that God is a Wise Steward? Because we can read about it in biblical Creation to learn the necessary stewardship principles and then imitate Him.

LOOK IT UP ↻

The words located throughout this book are essential. Use your Dictionary (D) or Thesaurus (T) to find their definitions. On a separate piece of paper, write down their descriptions. You will also find the above arrow on other pages to look up their meanings.

(The Answer Keys are on pages 68-74)

Action:

Budget:

Law:

Manager:

Owner:

Plan:

Principle: ***A truth, a law, or a rule for conduct.***

Steward:

Universal:

Wise:

Answer Key: Page 68

FIRST THINGS FIRST!!!

You are about to embark on the adventure of your life! Get ready to learn and understand the importance of stewardship principles found in Creation and how to use them in your life and with money!

It all begins with a __ __ __!

(find the word below to fill in the blanks above)

Effort Employment Job Labor Occupation Profession Work

On a separate sheet of paper, write down the above definition(s)

What does the Bible state about this requirement in II Thessalonians 3:10? Write it below.

Turn the page to see the Creation pattern and principles for you and me!

Answer Key: Page 68

DAY ONE

THE LIGHT

Genesis 1

1. In the beginning God created the heaven and the earth.

2. And the earth was without form, and void; and darkness was upon the face of the deep. And the Spirit of God moved upon the face of the waters.

3. And God said, Let there be light: and there was light.

4. And God saw the light, that it was good: and God divided the light from the darkness.

5. And God called the light Day, and the darkness he called Night. And the evening and the morning were the first day.

THE PRINCIPLE OF DAY ONE

GIVING FIRST

It is a Universal law

On the first day of Creation, when God said, "Let there be light" this implemented the primary stewardship principle of *Giving First*!

God loved us first, and He is the example we are to imitate. *(1 John 4:19)* We show our love to Him in many ways, such as praying first to Him in the morning. We must first learn to love ourselves so that we can love others.

We also show our love to God with our money. *(Matthew 6:21)* God has blessed us with many talents and abilities to earn money. After we receive our earnings, God wants us to show our thanks to Him by giving first to Him from our income.

Christians *give first* to God from their income with a tithe, meaning 10% of their earnings. In ancient times, a Tithe was called the First Fruits, which was 10% of the first and best from their harvest and animals.

The Tithe is one way to show God our gratitude and confidence for His continual blessings. *(Deuteronomy 12:6-7)* When we freely give the tithe, we should happily expect the benefits God promises to provide us in return. *(Malachi 3:10)*

When we Tithe, we are faithful to the stewardship Principle of Giving First!

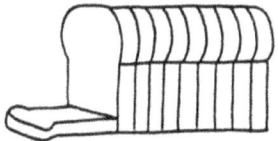

TITHES

Firstfruits, one-tenth, 10%, ten percent

Where we give our tithes is just as important. We bring our Tithe to our church, temple, synagogue, or wherever we attend services to receive our spiritual guidance. *(Deuteronomy 12:5-6)*

Tithes pay the pastors and priests salary to work full time in the ministry for their congregation's spiritual needs. *(Nehemiah 13:5)* They are then free to research, prepare sermons, visit and pray for sick members, and help others in the community. Tithes also pay staff to manage the business matters of the church.

The Bible states that those Christians who do not tithe are robbing God! *(Malachi 3:8-10)* Pastors and staff included. Robbing God is not tithing on the tithes given them or by mismanaging it. Ultimately, these pastors and staff will jeopardize the benefits of the Tithe. They could eventually lose their positions, jobs, and church.

When Christians do not tithe, it causes their families, churches, and communities to suffer needlessly.

TITHES DEFINITIONS:

Best   Contribution   First   Fruits   Gift   Ten Percent   Voluntary

THE PRINCIPLE: GIVING FIRST

Bestow   _____

_____

Contribute   _____

_____

Donate   _____

_____

Favor   _____

_____

Grant   _____

_____

Invest   _____

_____

Sacrifice   _____

_____

Answer Key: Page 68

SCRIPTURES FOR:

TITHES & GIVING FIRST

Honor the Lord with thy substance, and with the first fruits of all thine increase.
Proverbs 3:9

Bring ye all the tithes into the storehouse, that there may be meat in mine house, and prove me now herewith, saith the LORD of hosts, if I will not open you the windows of heaven, and pour you out a blessing, that there shall not be room enough to receive it.
Malachi 3:10

But woe unto you, Pharisees! for ye tithe mint and rue and all manner of herbs and pass over judgment and the love of God: these ought ye to have done, and not to leave the other undone.
Luke 11:42

HOW MUCH IS IT??

A wise steward looked at his earnings for four weeks to ensure that he correctly paid his Tithes. Each week was a different amount. He wanted to see his income after taxes and the difference between tithing on the Gross or the Net.

His tax rate is 20% on his weekly earnings.

Week	INCOME BEFORE TAXES	MINUS 20% TAXES	TAKE HOME PAY	MINUS 10% TITHES ON THE =GROSS=	AMOUNT LEFT FOR WEEKLY BUDGET
1.	$1,000	-$200	**$800**	**-$ 100**	$700
2.	$1,200	-$240	**$960**	**-$ 120**	$840
3.	$1,100	-$220	**$880**	**-$ 110**	$770
4.	$1,050	-$210	**$840**	**-$105**	$735

Week	INCOME BEFORE TAXES	MINUS 20% TAXES	TAKE HOME PAY	MINUS 10% TITHES ON THE =NET=	AMOUNT LEFT FOR WEEKLY BUDGET
1.	$1,000	-$200	**$800**	**-$80**	$720
2.	$1,200	--$240	**$960**	**-$96**	$864
3.	$1,100	-$220	**$880**	**-$88**	$792
4.	$1,050	-$210	**$840**	**-$84**	$756

Subtract the dollar difference between tithing on the gross and the net.

Week 1. _____   Week 2 _____   Week 3. _____   Week 4. _____

Answer Key: Page 68

DAY TWO

THE HEAVEN

Genesis 1

6. And God said, Let there be a firmament in the midst of the waters, and let it divide the waters from the waters.

7. And God made the firmament, and divided the waters which were under the firmament from the waters which were above the firmament: and it was so.

8. And God called the firmament Heaven. And the evening and the morning were the second day.

THE PRINCIPLE OF DAY TWO

OBEDIENCE TO AUTHORITY

It is a Universal law

On this day, God instituted the stewardship principle of Authority, but more specifically, Obedience to Authority.

God's plans were for a heavenly government filled with angel stewards and an earthly government filled with human stewards. In both governments, God expects Obedience to Authority from angels and mankind. *(Matthew 6:10; Romans 13:1)*

All countries require their citizens to be Obedient to Authority and obey the laws. By law, citizens must pay taxes. The Bible states that we are to pay taxes to *"whomever they are due." (Romans 13:7)*

Of course, no one pays taxes in Heaven, but everyone in heaven and earth must be Obedient to Authority. If they don't, they will suffer unfortunate consequences, whether in heaven or earth. *(Genesis 3:14-24; Matthew 5:25-26; Luke 10:18)*

Whenever there are unfaithful stewards in authoritative positions, God changes those leaders as <u>He</u> decides and through whomever He chooses. *(Isaiah 14:12; Daniel 2:21; Rev 12:7-9)*

When we pay taxes to our government, we are faithful to the stewardship principle of Obedience to Authority!

TAXES

Financial support for a nation; a government's treasury paid by its citizens

A nation's government collects taxes from its citizens' income to provide the necessities and resources for its cities and states' needs. Citizens pay taxes through various means, like sales tax, business tax, property tax, income tax, and many other taxes.

Governments distribute tax money for their citizen's needs such as education, healthcare, security, libraries, bridges, medical research, and more. Taxes also pay government employees' salaries who depend upon the tax money to take care of their families.

If citizens fail to pay their taxes, they will incur penalties and fines that add to their tax bill. On occasion, some end up going to jail for not paying their taxes or fraudulently withholding them.

Tax administrators must also be wise stewards and maintain balanced budgets. They also must be trustworthy stewards and carefully budget and administer the monies where needed. They should never fraudulently abuse tax monies, their positions, or their employees.

Not paying taxes causes families and citizens in communities, cities, states, and nations to suffer needlessly. *(Proverbs 29:2)*

TAXES DEFINITIONS:

Assess   Charge   Custom   Duty   Revenue   Tariff   Toll

THE PRINCIPLE: OBEDIENCE TO AUTHORITY

Allegiance: _____

_____

Authority: _____

_____

Comply: _____

_____

Loyalty: _____

_____

Obey: _____

_____

Respect: _____

_____

Submission: _____

_____

Answer Key: Page 69

SCRIPTURES FOR:

TAXES & OBEDIENCE TO AUTHORITY

Thy kingdom come, thy will be done in earth, as it is in heaven.
Matthew 6:10

Let every soul be subject unto the higher powers. For there is no power but of God: the powers that be are ordained of God.
Romans 13:1

Render therefore to all their dues: tribute to whom tribute is due; custom to whom custom; fear to whom fear; honour to whom honour.
Romans 13:7

Taxes Paid with Money from Around the World

Which countries do they represent?

Answer Key: Page 69

DAY THREE

SEAS, EARTH, VEGETATION, SEEDS

Genesis 1

9. And God said, Let the waters under the heaven be gathered together unto one place, and let the dry land appear: and it was so.

10. And God called the dry land Earth; and the gathering together of the waters called he Seas: and God saw that it was good.

11. And God said, Let the earth bring forth grass, the herb yielding seed, and the fruit tree yielding fruit after his kind, whose seed is in itself, upon the earth: and it was so.

12. And the earth brought forth grass, and herb yielding seed after his kind, and the tree yielding fruit, whose seed was in itself, after his kind: and God saw that it was good.

13. And the evening and the morning were the third day.

THE PRINCIPLE OF DAY THREE

CONTINUITY

It is a Universal law

On this day, through seeds, we are faithful to the stewardship principle of Continuity. Continuity means cycles of regular and recurring events.

When we plant seeds, not only do they reproduce themselves, but once they mature, they also produce many more seeds. Seeds benefit the ones who plant them, whoever harvests their produce, all who eat the produce, and again, the ones who replant the seeds. The Bible states that as long as there is an Earth, seedtime and harvest will never end. *(Genesis 8:22)*

Continuity also works with our money. When we give financial offerings to places like churches, synagogues, and temples, it helps with its maintenance and monthly bills. Offerings enable them to remain open and available to everyone.

No one must attend a church to give an offering. Nor do offerings have to be a certain amount of money or a percentage of one's income. Offerings should be an amount that someone gives <u>willingly</u>. *(Exodus 35:5)*. Like seeds, offerings benefit the one who gives it, and the one who receives it, who is then able to provide an offering too! *(Luke 6:38)*

When we give offerings, we are faithful to the stewardship principle of Continuity.

OFFERINGS

Free, continual gift of aid and support; an act of worship

Much like our homes' needs, offerings pay the monthly bills, mortgage, maintenance, repair, and other church necessities. Some of the offerings help a network of other organizations within the community that also serve others.

Once or twice a year, pastors will ask for a special offering, called Alms, to aid the extremely poor and destitute. However, Alms are additional freewill offerings. The Bible states that when we give Alms, it is the same as lending to the Lord, and He promises to repay those who give it. *(Proverbs19:17; Matthew 6:1, 4)*

Offerings must also be managed wisely by pastors and their staff; else, it will cause their own families, church, congregation, and the community to suffer needlessly.

OFFERINGS DEFINITIONS:

Allot   Generous   Gift   Furnish   Present   Supply   Voluntary

THE PRINCIPLE: CONTINUITY

Ceaseless: _____

_____

Continuous: _____

_____

Cycle: _____

_____

Repeat: _____

_____

Recur: _____

_____

Series: _____

_____

Successive: _____

_____

Answer Key: Page 69

SCRIPTURES FOR:

CONTINUITY & OFFERINGS

Whosoever is of a willing heart, let him bring it, an offering unto the Lord.
Exodus 35:5

Every man shall give as he is able, according to the blessing of the Lord thy God which he hath given thee.
Deuteronomy 16:17

Every man according as he purposeth in his heart, so let him give; not grudgingly, or of necessity: For God loveth a cheerful giver.
II *Corinthians 9:7*

BAD OFFERINGS

There's a Biblical story about people who were required to bring animal offerings to the Priests for their Temple service. However, the people brought animal offerings that were torn, blind, lame, and sick.

The torn animals were maimed; lame animals had deformities or were injured; sick animals were diseased, and blind animals were sightless from birth or accident. Rather than destroy these animals, and against their better judgment, the people brought these unsatisfactory offerings to the temple.

The priests depended on offerings* from the people to provide food for their families. Even though the Priests angrily accepted it, they were still angry when they offered it to God and complained that it didn't do them any good to serve God, just to receive bad offerings. *(Malachi 3:13-15)*

God was angry with the people and the priests because they dared to offer Him angry, despicable, and imperfect offerings instead of perfect freewill offerings. God sent a prophet to warn them of their misdeeds and gave them another chance to correct their attitudes and offerings. *(Malachi 1:6-14)*

An example of bad financial offerings today is similar to this story.

1. <u>**Torn Offering**</u>
   This offering is when a Christian can give it but refuses to do so, or in anger, give a stingy amount. It is the same as giving money "torn" from their hands. (It could also be not giving the full tithe).

2. **Lame Offering**

   Offerings form the church's yearly budget, so a Lame offering is when anyone makes a vow to give but fails to complete it. Their inaction causes the church to limp along and struggle financially.

3. **Sick Offering**

   Mismanaged money is considered a sick offering. Some people haphazardly spend their paycheck, and afterward, although they want to give offerings, they have nothing left or very little to offer. They are embarrassed and often sorry, yet repeatedly do the same thing each paycheck. They never make a budget to include offerings, and they don't pay their bills on time, if at all.

4. **Blind Offering**

   This offering is money someone promises to give "someday," but they never try to accomplish it. In essence, the church will never see it! Offerings are not that important to them, so whenever it's time to give an offering, they reply, "Not Yet! Not Yet!"

When pastors and priests present our offerings to the Lord, it is required to give them with love, gratitude, and a willing heart. No one should offer God torn, lame, sick, or blind offerings. Thankfully, God allows us to repent, forgives us, and help change our attitude and heart.

What other offering types did the people bring to the temple?

Answer Key: Page 69

DAY FOUR

THE SUN, MOON, STARS

14. And God said, Let there be lights in the firmament of the heaven to divide the day from the night, and let them be for signs, and for seasons, and for days, and years:

15. And let them be for lights in the firmament of the heaven to give light upon the earth: and it was so.

16. And God made two great lights; the greater light to rule the day, and the lesser light to rule the night: he made the stars also.

17. And God set them in the firmament of the heaven to give light upon the earth,

18. And to rule over the day and over the night, and to divide the light from the darkness: and God saw that it was good.

19. And the evening and the morning were the fourth day.

THE PRINCIPLE OF DAY FOUR

PREPARATION

It is a Universal law

On this day, God instituted the stewardship principle of Preparation for the times and seasons of life.

Days add up to weeks, weeks add up to months, and months add up to years for every living thing. We all must prepare for our needs *"ahead of time, and ahead of the need."*

Preparation in our finances is by saving money *"ahead of time, and ahead of the need."* One must save money for themselves, short-term goals, large expenses, seasonal events, and especially for unexpected emergencies.

Everyone's needs begin before birth, at birth, through teenage years, adulthood, working years, retirement, and even one's death. Preparations must be made for it all.

Over time, when saving and investing money, its value should grow through interest and reinvesting. The more one understands the significance of money as a tool for bettering themselves and others; it will be a lifelong guide. It's never too early or too late to learn about successful financial tools.

When we save money, we are faithful to the stewardship principle of Preparation.

SAVINGS

To prepare, reserve, or set aside something of value for future events; bank or storehouse

There are many ways to save money, such as piggy banks, bank accounts, stocks, and other investments. One should save money for items they would like to have in the future, such as college tuition, marriage, children, houses, or whatever else they desire. However, one should always have more than one savings account because unexpected emergencies often happen when least expected. *(Ecclesiastes 11:2)*

It's wise to save money throughout the year for holidays, yearly celebrations, and events in which families love to participate. It is also best to save for retirement long before it happens. Burial insurance is also a savings account. People should save for how they want to be buried - *ahead of time and ahead of the need.*

Everyone must save money "*ahead of time, and ahead of the need*" for seasonal events so they can purchase necessities for each season. If one lives in a place where the season temperatures vary throughout the year, they must prepare for it ***before*** it occurs.

Governments and churches should also save money "*ahead of time, and ahead of the need.*" They have growth needs and unexpected emergencies for their citizens. Pastors and staff must also save for the future needs of its building, member growth or decline, and preserving its future in the community.

When people do not save money "*ahead of time, and ahead of the need,*" it causes families, churches, communities, and governments to suffer needlessly.

SAVINGS DEFINITIONS

Accumulate   Bank   Conserve   Deposit   Reserve   Treasure

THE PRINCIPLE: PREPARATION

Anticipate: _____

_____

Arrange: _____

_____

Equip: _____

_____

Expect: _____

_____

Prepare: _____

_____

Precaution: _____

_____

Ready: _____

_____

Answer Key: Page 70

SCRIPTURES FOR

PREPARATION & SAVINGS

Give a portion to seven, and also to eight; for thou knowest not what evil shall be upon the earth.
Ecclesiastes 11:2

Blessed shall be thy basket and thy store.
Deuteronomy 28:5

Lord, thou deliveredst unto me five talents; behold, I have gained beside them five talents more. His Lord said unto him, Well done, thou good and faithful servant..."
Matthew 25:20-21

A-MAZE-MENT

This story is about a wise steward and a lazy steward. Both hid some of their money in a cave filled with a maze of caverns. Some of the caverns were safe, and some were lethal.

The wise steward worked, saved, and invested his money. He continually learned new skills and followed his budget to meet his financial goals. When he got a job, he paid his bills, saved his money, bought a house, and vacationed wherever he wanted. He stored his extra money in the cave behind a locked gate with his secret code. Even though he had some unexpected financial difficulties along the way, he adjusted his budget as necessary and accomplished his financial goals.

The lazy steward worked occasionally but loved to spend much of his money on frivolous things. He was too lazy to make a budget. Whatever money was left, he also hid it behind his locked gate with a secret code - *X marks the spot!*

Unfortunately, the lazy steward forgot his secret code. He later remembered that he built a brick wall in front of where he hid his money! Even if he could get in, he couldn't break down the wall! Rather than find a job, he constantly worried about his hidden money. Depressed and upset, he refused to go back to work and sat beneath a palm tree waiting for something to happen. Sadly, he ended up begging for food and slept on the streets!

Search the maze of caverns to see if either steward could get their money and get back out without entering a lethal cavern.

THE STEWARD'S MAZE

There are five lethal caverns in the maze. Draw a line through the caverns to get to the money and then get back out without ending up in a lethal one. Once you enter it, you cannot escape!

1. Which ones are the Lethal caverns?
2. What circumstances can the Lethal caverns represent? Example: Addiction to anything!
3. Did the Wise Steward find a way to his money?
4. Did the Lazy Steward find a way to his money?

Answer Key: *Page 70*

DAY FIVE

THE FISH & BIRDS

Genesis 1

20. And God said, Let the waters bring forth abundantly the moving creature that hath life, and fowl that may fly above the earth in the open firmament of heaven.

21. And God created great whales, and every living creature that moveth, which the waters brought forth abundantly, after their kind, and every winged fowl after his kind: and God saw that it was good.

22. And God blessed them, saying, Be fruitful, and multiply, and fill the waters in the seas, and let fowl multiply in the earth.

23. And the evening and the morning were the fifth day.

THE PRINCIPLE OF DAY FIVE

PROVISION

It is a Universal law

On this day, God instituted the stewardship principle of Provision *before* He created the first species of fish and birds.

God already provided their habitats when He created the seas and the earth where they were to live and created the green herbs for their food. *(Genesis 1:30)* God also blessed them with seeds within themselves to reproduce their species every year.

Ideally, people should provide for their own basic needs *before* becoming parents. By first working and providing for themselves, they will learn and understand how and why to provide food, clothing, and shelter for themselves and their future family.

Parents must also provide a safe environment for their families inside and outside the home. Home is the place that should provide love, support, pride, peace, and self-confidence that children need to live, mature, survive, and thrive. By their parent's example, children will learn what it means to be a wise parent, along with a variety of other resources available in libraries to help teach them. *(Proverbs 22:6)*

Although the cost of living goes up each year, basic needs never change, and businesses depend upon neighborhood families to buy their basic needs and supplies from them. These businesses likewise provide jobs for people in the neighborhood so they too can care for their families.

When we provide for our household, we are faithful to the stewardship principle of Provision.

FAMILY

Kin; persons related by blood or marriage; household members; relationships

Home is where children first learn and understand how to love, share, care for themselves, and nurture others. *(Psalms 127:1-5)*

As children develop natural talents, skills, and abilities, parents should identify them while observing their limitations. Parents can then nurture, guide, and encourage their children to use their skills to become responsible adults.

Children also should have meaningful chores and learn to complete them on time, long before they begin a paying job. They will also need to know what education or specific training is necessary for the job or profession they choose and the money they can expect to earn from it. They need to understand that if they want to live the same lifestyle as they do now or a different one in the future, it requires knowing these skills.

As children mature, they must learn how to set goals, budget time, and manage their own money. Recreation must also be a part of this training. When parents participate in recreational activities with their children, it helps them learn to respect their family and others.

If parents don't provide life's necessities and recreation for themselves and their family, it causes families, churches, government, and communities to suffer needlessly.

FAMILY DEFINITIONS

Ancestors   Family   Descendants   Genealogy   Parents   Children   Clan

THE PRINCIPLE: PROVISION

Furnish: _____

_____

Obligation: _____

_____

Provide: _____

_____

Provision: _____

_____

Responsible: _____

_____

Require: _____

_____

Supply: _____

_____

Answer Key: Page 71

SCRIPTURES FOR:

PROVISION & FAMILY

God setteth the solitary in families...
Psalm 68:6

She looketh well to the ways of her household...Her children arise up, and call her blessed; her husband also, and he praiseth her. Many daughters have done virtuously, but thou excellest them all.
Proverbs 31:27-29

But if any provide not for his own, and especially for those of his own house, he hath denied the faith, and is worse than an infidel.
I Timothy 5:8

THE STEWARD'S BUDGET

A steward just got a job and wanted to be generous, but he only estimated a budget based on his Gross paycheck of $2,500. Unfortunately, his estimates are all wrong. He constantly overspends his salary, mismanages his money, and cannot figure out why.

He forgot that his taxes were 20% of his income, which is deducted first from every paycheck, leaving him a Net income of $2,000. He plans on not paying some bills, and he doesn't want to tithe or give offerings anymore.

On the next page, help him make the necessary adjustments to his budget by using his **Net** income of $2,000. He will have to sacrifice some things for a while to get back on a budget. Some household costs remain the same, like the Mortgage or Rent.

If he tithes or gives offerings, he must decide if he's going to base it on his Gross or Net income. Since he absolutely cannot give 10% for Tithes, budget for another amount, like 1%, until he can increase it to 10%. It's always his decision of what, if any, he decides to give as an offering. The only requirement is that he gives it with gratitude!

As the Steward pays off some of his bills or his income increases, he can use the extra money towards other bills. If he hasn't spent all of his recreational cash, he can add it to Savings since it's his Surplus money. Always plan something for Recreation, even if it's renting a movie or making a fun meal at home. Be sure to decide on something interesting!

Adjust the budget as necessary rather than skip paying bills.

Remember: *Create the budget from the **Net** salary!!!*

FIX THE STEWARD'S BUDGET

Gross Wages $2,500	Net Income after 20% Taxes $2,000	Net Income After 20% Tax $2,000
TAXES	*500*	*500*
TITHES	**If Tithe paid on the Gross** 250	**If Tithe paid on Net** 200
OFFERINGS*		
SAVINGS**		
HOUSEHOLD COSTS		
MORTGAGE/RENT	600	600
GAS/ELECTRICITY		
GROCERIES		
PHONE-CELL		
CABLE T.V.		
TRANSPORTATION		
MEDICAL		
MISCELLANEOUS		
CHARITY		
SURPLUS		
TOTALS	Must Total $2,000	Must Total $2,000

*Any offering amount that you decide
** Any savings amount that you decide

Answer Key: Page 71

DAY SIX

ANIMALS & MAN

Genesis 1

24. And God said, Let the earth bring forth the living creature after his kind, cattle, and creeping thing, and beast of the earth after his kind: and it was so.

25. And God made the beast of the earth after his kind, and cattle after their kind, and every thing that creepeth upon the earth after his kind: and God saw that it was good.

26. And God said, Let us make man in our image, after our likeness: and let them have dominion over the fish of the sea, and over the fowl of the air, and over the cattle, and over all the earth, and over every creeping thing that creepeth upon the earth.

27. So God created man in his own image, in the image of God created he him; male and female created he them.

28. And God blessed them, and God said unto them, Be fruitful, and multiply, and replenish the earth, and subdue it: and have dominion over the fish of the sea, and over the fowl of the air, and over every living thing that moveth upon the earth.

29. And God said, Behold, I have given you every herb bearing seed, which is upon the face of all the earth, and every tree, in the which is the fruit of a tree yielding seed; to you it shall be for meat.

30. And to every beast of the earth, and to every fowl of the air, and to every thing that creepeth upon the earth, wherein there is life, I have given every green herb for meat: and it was so.

31. And God saw every thing that he had made, and, behold, it was very good. And the evening and the morning were the sixth day.

THE PRINCIPLE OF DAY SIX

UNCONDITIONAL LOVE

It is a Universal law

On this day, God instituted the stewardship principle of Unconditional Love. God unselfishly shared Himself unconditionally with the man by making him *in His very own image and likeness.* God created man as an earthly replica of what He looks like in the Spirit.

Before He created man, he made the animals first to assist man. By caring for the animals, the man learned how to love and care for something other than himself. Afterward, God made a woman and brought her to the man as his mate. They, too, had seeds within themselves to reproduce their species and imitate the principle of Unconditional Love towards each other.

God then gave mankind dominion (stewardship) to care for and protect all the other things He created, like the environments of the sky, land, seas, vegetation, fish, birds, and animals. All of Creation is connected because everything is necessary for our survival.

After providing for one's own family and children, individuals and families can share Unconditional Love with others who have suffered a sudden hardship. Disasters happen locally and worldwide to people, animals, and their environments. Individuals and families can include in their budget a small amount of money to share with those who do not know them nor can repay them for their kindness.

Adults who respond to disasters with empathy and kindness demonstrate to children what compassion and unselfishness mean. It will help them be thankful for what they have, who they are as a family, and proud of themselves.

When we share, we are faithful to the stewardship principle of Unconditional Love.

SHARING

A part or portion of something;
the dividing of a larger share

Unexpected or unforeseen tragedies happen anytime, whether it's people, animals, or habitats, and people can demonstrate Unconditional Love with them by sharing. When disasters occur, financial donations, large or small, can be given to charities, churches, or other organizations that provide food, water, shelter, clothes to those in these situations.

Individuals and families can review various organizations and mission groups to decide how much to share and with whom to share it. Whatever a person or family decides, a small amount of money can be shared with others once a year, quarterly, or monthly.

Besides sharing food or money, there are volunteer mission groups like doctors, nurses, pastors, and others willing to share their medical knowledge, faith, time, and Bibles with cultures worldwide. Rather than becoming a volunteer, anyone can donate to finance these volunteer groups' expenses.

When we do not share with others, it causes people in our families, neighborhoods, nation, and the world to suffer needlessly.

SHARING DEFINITIONS:

Allotment   Assign   Dole   Distribute   Divide   Parcel   Part

THE PRINCIPLE: UNCONDITIONAL LOVE

Absolute: _____

_____

Complete: _____

_____

Free: _____

_____

Loving: _____

_____

Perfect: _____

_____

Unlimited: _____

_____

Vast: _____

_____

Answer Key: Page 72

SCRIPTURES FOR:

UNCONDITIONAL LOVE & SHARING

And God said, Let us make man in our image, After our likeness…
Genesis 1:26

....Thou shalt love thy neighbor as thyself.
Matthew 22:39

…Go ye into all the world, and preach the gospel...
Mark 16:15

BUILDING BLOCKS
FOR SHARING

It is always your choice to share with anyone you desire, or you can give the entire amount to one charity. Begin with the needs in your neighborhood, local community, or city. *Every Wise Steward should research a charity's background before choosing to give to them.* There are many to choose from other than the ones listed below.

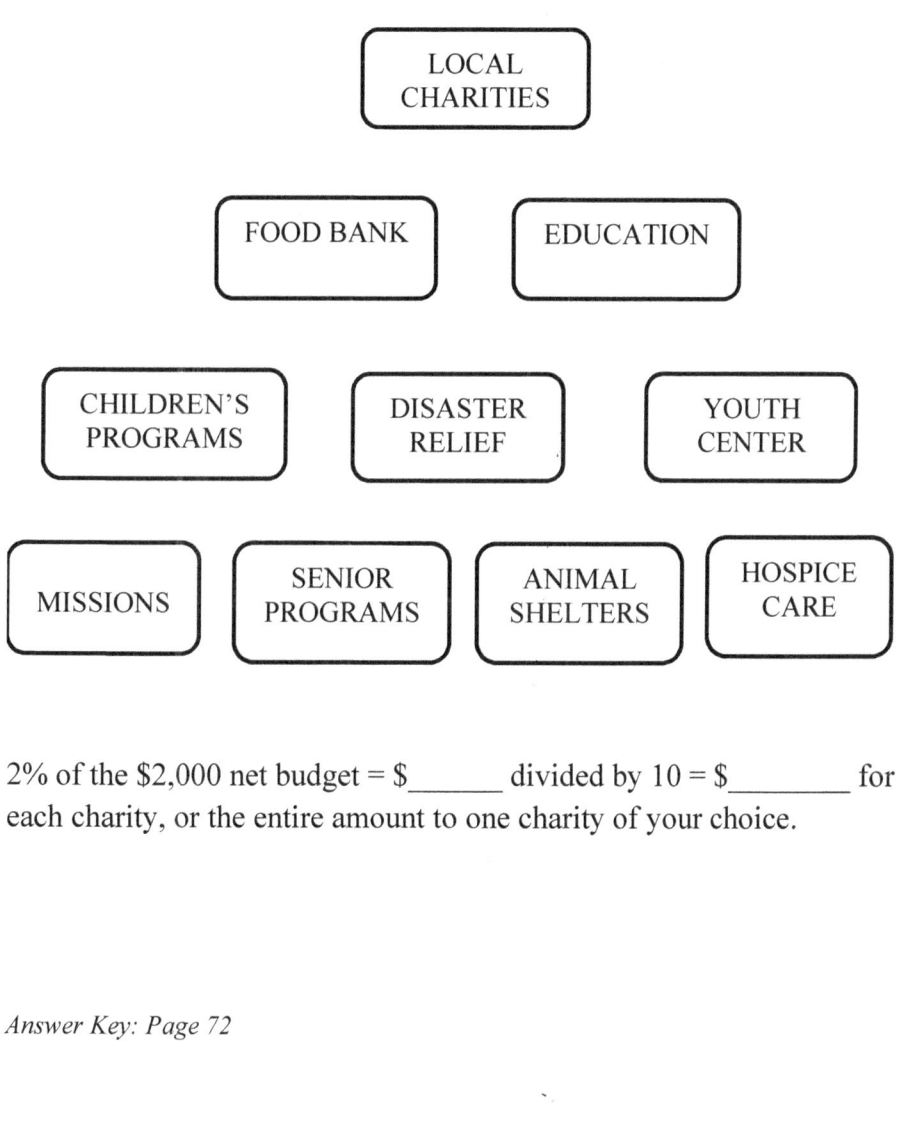

2% of the $2,000 net budget = $_____ divided by 10 = $_____ for each charity, or the entire amount to one charity of your choice.

Answer Key: Page 72

DAY SEVEN

REST

Genesis 2

1. Thus the heavens and the earth were finished, and all the host of them.

2. And on the seventh day God ended his work which he had made; and he rested on the seventh day from all his work which he had made.

3. And God blessed the seventh day, and sanctified it: because that in it he had rested from all his work which God created and made.

THE PRINCIPLE OF DAY SEVEN

BALANCE

It is a Universal law

After six days, God finished creating. He rested on the seventh day, instituting the stewardship principle of Balance.

It's not healthy to work or play all the time, so everyone "must budget" a time to relax and enjoy a quiet time just to themselves. This time does not include family, job, church, or anyone else. Individual relaxation or Balance enables one to appreciate themselves, their family, job, and life. After we rest, we can look forward to each day and see the good in others and all situations. *(Psalm 128:1-2)*

Wise stewards understand that they must have a Balance in their money. They realize that they should not leave themselves out of their budget. How much money should be decided upon and entered into the budget, because no one is ever to give away all their hard-earned money to everything and everyone else.

People who wisely manage their obligations can relax and be at peace with themselves because they have earned an income, successfully budgeted their priorities and commitments, and accomplished their financial responsibilities. Wise stewards, when rested, will not suffer needlessly.

When we rest, we are faithful to the stewardship principle of Balance.

SURPLUS

Excess, remaining;
beyond what is necessary

Before creating a budget, and after considering all other financial obligations, the person who earns an income is the one who decides how much should be set aside just for themselves! It is called Surplus money. This money can be used for personal hobbies, entertainment, buying something for themselves, or not spend at all.

Also, a person must balance time each day to not use it for anything else. Before or after work, but before retiring for a good night's sleep, a person should set aside time for themselves to enjoy a relaxing activity. It doesn't matter if they read, watch television, exercise, jog, nap, shop, or any activity that's enjoyable to them.

Maintaining a balance between work and play helps people stay focused on life's true riches - their spiritual well-being, self-worth, family, health, and employment. It is very satisfying when one knows that they have been a wise and faithful steward over all that has been entrusted to them to love, care, and protect.

If anyone gives to everyone and everything else yet neglects themselves, unfortunately, all other relationships <u>will suffer</u> needlessly!

SURPLUS DEFINITIONS:

Additional   Increase   Gain   Leftover   Profit   Return   Sufficient

THE PRINCIPLE: BALANCE

Adjust: _____

_____

Balanced: _____

_____

Harmony: _____

_____

Peaceful: _____

_____

Remainder: _____

_____

Rest: _____

_____

Stability: _____

_____

Answer Key: Page 72

SCRIPTURES FOR:

BALANCE & SURPLUS

He maketh me to lie down in green pastures; …He restoreth my soul:
Psalm 23:2-3a

The blessing of the Lord, it maketh rich, and he addeth no sorrow with it.
Proverbs 10:22

There remaineth therefore a rest to the people of God.
Hebrews 4:9

DEPUTIES NEEDED
Apply Immediately

An unwise Steward lost his Surplus money. The Sheriff needs several deputies to help find it. Only those experienced in Wise Stewardship Principles need to apply!

WANTED

LOST:	**SURPLUS MONEY**
BY:	**AN UNWISE STEWARD**
WHEN:	**LAST PAYCHECK**
IF FOUND:	**RETURN TO BUDGET**
REWARD:	**PEACE OF MIND**

STEWARDSHIP FINAL REVIEW

EXAMPLE: Day 1: LIGHT

Principle: Giving First, **Stewardship**: Tithes, **Scripture**: Malachi 3:10
Visual:

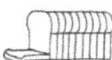

II.   Necessary Action for the Tithes Principle:

Effort   Employment   Job   Labor   Occupation   Profession   Work

III.   The meaning of the Tithes Principle:

Bestow   Contribute   Donate   Favor   Grant   Invest   Sacrifice

IV. All Seven Stewardship Financial Responsibilities:

1. Tithes 2. Taxes 3. Offerings 4. Savings 5. Family 6. Sharing 7. Surplus

V. All Seven Principles for Stewardship Financial Responsibilities:

1.   Giving First
2.   Obedience to Authority
3.   Continuity
4.   Preparation
5.   Provision
6.   Unconditional Love
7.   Balance

VI. All Seven Visuals:

1. 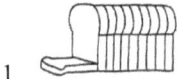   2.    3.    4.

5.    6.    7.

CAN YOU HANDLE IT?

*The Following Worksheets Are Designed
to Understand Wise Stewardship*

IN THE DARK

Darken the K's, Q's, V's, and Z's in the boxes below to find out the description of:

A WISE STEWARD

Answer Key: Page 72

WORD SEARCH

Find the following words:

Tithes Taxes Offerings Savings Family Sharing Surplus

BONUS WORD: Wise

B	F	A	C	D	E	F	G	S
S	A	V	I	N	G	S	H	T
G	Y	L	I	M	A	F	E	A
N	E	T	A	X	E	S	O	R
I	R	S	U	L	P	R	U	S
R	S	I	O	N	S	O	W	U
E	T	T	N	E	C	R	I	P
F	T	I	T	H	E	S	S	L
F	F	W	L	X	O	T	E	R
O	P	S	H	A	R	I	N	G

Answer Key: Page 73

STEWARD-SHIP-WRECK

This steward forgot the stewardship principles, and his budget is all messed up. His life is a wreck! Draw a line to match the correct **Principle** with its picture. Then draw a line to its proper **Action**.

PRINCIPLE	VISUAL	WISE STEWARD ACTION
Balance		Sharing
Unconditional Love		Savings
Preparation		Offerings
Provision		Taxes
Obedience to Authority		Tithes
Continuity		Family
Giving First		Surplus

Answer Key: Page 74

HIDDEN TAX LETTER

The Taxman left a phone message for an unwise steward, advising him to come to his office to discuss his taxable earnings. For some reason, the unwise steward's earnings did not match up to his spending.

The unwise steward did not want to go to the Taxman's office, so he wrote him a letter. Deceitfully, the unwise steward hid his taxes in the letter. Search the letter below to find the 11 hidden taxes. Underline them.

Dear Mr. Tax Man:

I received your phone message regarding my taxes. I took a taxicab to your office to discuss it, but apparently, I had the wrong address. I ended up at a Taxidermist office. The time and money I spent doing this, left me overtaxed and tired, so I returned home. Again, I looked at my taxable income, and as a taxpayer, I feel that I should not have any unnecessary surtaxes charged to me because of your error. Please pardon my grammar syntax, as I am very upset that you want to discuss these taxation issues with me.

Sincerely,

An Overtaxed Steward

Answer Key: Page 74

UNSCRAMBLE

A Wise Steward hired a financial steward to help him manage his money. The Wise Steward was away on vacation, so he wrote the financial steward a letter listing what he wanted to be done with his money while he was away. However, the financial steward was confused because he could not understand the words in his client's letter. The financial steward knows you are a Wise Steward and needs your help to interpret the letter.

Using the stewardship principles, unscramble the words so that the financial steward will know what the Wise Steward wants him to do.

Dear Financial Steward,

While I am away on vacation, please handle the following business matters precisely as I have outlined below.

1. Send my hettis to my church.
2. Pay my xatse I owe to the government.
3. Send my feforinsg to my church.
4. Put $1,000 into my various vasnigs accounts.
5. Pay my miafly bills, including what I owe you.
6. haser to a children's charity in my community.
7. Mail my plsursu check to me so I can use it on vacation.

Once you have completed these tasks, be sure to mail me copies of all receipts. Thank you.

Sincerely,

A Wise Steward

Answer Key: Page 74

IT'S ONLY A TEST!

Ask someone in your family to allow YOU to figure out what the Tithes are from their paycheck each week or month. *You are not to ask if they paid them.*

You may also figure it out by using your allowance.

Remember: This is something that YOU must plan for, practice, and adjust as necessary with the NET income.

Notice: *Each paycheck is different each payday!*

	Paycheck Before Taxes Gross Amount	Paycheck After Taxes Net Amount	10% Tithes if Paid on the Gross Paycheck	10% Tithes if Paid on the Net Paycheck	What is the $ Difference Between Paying on the Gross or the Net
1.	$	$	$	$	$
2.	$	$	$	$	$
3.	$	$	$	$	$
4.	$	$	$	$	$

CREATE YOUR OWN STORY

Make as many copies as you need for this project. Draw your pictures in the letters. Next, write a story about it. An example might be:

W = I have two ice cream cones
A = I erected a Teepee in the backyard

Next, print your name in large letters on another piece of paper. Draw pictures inside the letters of your name and make up a story.

T

R

D

MY FUTURE OCCUPATION

The following two pages are personal. <u>YOU</u> must locate the answers. You can search the internet, go to a library, school counselor, or obtain a college handbook.

1. When I grow up, I want to become a:

2. I want to work at this job because:

3. I can expect to earn this amount of money from my profession: (do not guess)

Your Profession Earns How Much?

- Per Year: \$_____ (minus 20% taxes) = \$_____

- Per week \$_____ (minus 20% taxes) = \$_____

- Per month \$_____ (minus 20% taxes) = \$_____

RESEARCH ASSIGNMENT

1. Will you need an education for this occupation?

2. If so, how long will it take to complete your education?

3. How much will your education cost?

- College: Tuition x 4-6 years (or more) $_____

- Trade School: Tuition x 1-3 years (or more) $_____

- Books: Per class x 1-6 years (or more) $_____

- Dorm Room: Rent + Food x 4-6 years $_____

TOTALS $_____

4. How will you pay for it if your parents can't pay for it?

5. Will your grades qualify you for a scholarship or grant?

6. Will you have to know Math, English, or Science for this occupation?

7. Will it matter if you have a criminal background? Why or why not?

8. If yes, will you have to choose another profession?

9. Do you know someone employed in this occupation?

NOTES:

What are the most important things you learned about being a Wise Steward from the Six Days of Creation and Rest? What surprised you? List it below.

1.

2.

3.

4.

5.

6.

7.

ANSWER KEY

(D) Dictionary   (T) Thesaurus

Page 9   LOOK IT UP
Action: (D) activity (T) movement, response, work
Budget: (D) income to expenses (T) operation costs, plan
Manager: (D) manages a business (T) director, supervisor
Plan: (D) an outline (T) map, chart, timeline, roadmap
Principle: (D) a rule of conduct, a truth, law (T) belief system
Steward: (D) finance administrator (T) agent, manager
Universal: (D) everywhere; used by all (T) worldwide, total
Wise: (D) good judgment; informed (T) sensible smart

Page 10   FIRST THINGS FIRST!!
J-O-B

Effort: (D) attempt, try, work (T) enterprise, struggle
Employment: (D) job, profession, vocation (T) work
Job: (D) employment, profession (T) gainful work
Labor   (D) physical movement, tasks (T) toil, activity
Occupation: (D) work, profession (T) craft, trade
Profession   (D) job, training (T) skilled occupation
Work: (D) effort, labor, toil (T) task, obligation

II Thessalonians 3:10 "...this we commanded you, that if any
would not work, neither should he eat

Page 14   *TITHES DEFINITIONS*
Bestow: (D) present, gift; offer, give (T) bequeath
Contribute: (D) give jointly, (T) share, give away, donate
Donate: (D) give or contribute (T) provide, grant
Favor: (D) kind, support (T) prefer, praise, esteem
Grant   (D) give, transfer (T) gift, reward, donation
Invest   (D) for profit (T) give money into person/thing
Sacrifice   (D) give up something for another (T) tribute

Page 16   HOW MUCH IS IT?
Week 1. $20   Week 2. $24   3. $22   Week 4. $21

Answer Key Continued

Page 20   TAX DEFINITIONS
Allegiance: (D) duty/loyalty to country, devotion (T) homage
Authority: (D) command, influence (T) prestige, power
Comply: (D) act on an order (T) consent, yield, obey
Loyalty: (D) faithfulness (T) trustworthy, dependable
Obey: (D) complete orders (T) submit, consent
Respect: (D) honor, esteem (T) value, admire, courtesy
Submission: (D) yielding control to another (T) meekness

Page 22   TAXES PAID WITH MONEY FROM AROUND THE WORLD
Dinar: Iraq
Dollar: United States, and other countries
Euro: European Nations
Krone: Denmark, Greenland, and Faroe Islands
Peso: Latin American countries and the Philippines
Pound: United Kingdom, England
Riyal: Saudi Arabia
Ruble: Russia
Shekel: Israel
Yen: Japan
Won: South Korea

Page 26   OFFERINGS DEFINITIONS
Ceaseless: (D) continual (T) endless, unending, eternal
Continuity: (D) unbroken, whole (T) constant, unity, sequence
Cycle: (D) regular recurring events; completed (T) time
Repeat: (D) do again (T) redo, remake, renew
Recur: (D) occur again, (T) reappear, crop up, repeat
Series   (D) occurring in a row (T) sequence, continuity
Successive: (D) one after the other (T) serial, in-line

Page 29   *OTHER OFFERINGS:
Gemstones, wood, animal skins, cloth, incense, ointment, flour,
oil, salt, wheat

Answer Key Continued

Page 33   SAVINGS DEFINITIONS
Anticipate: (D) in advance (T) forecast, predict
Arrange: (D) put in correct order, prepare, (T) make ready
Equip: (D) provide what is needed, (T) furnish, supply
Expect: (D) likely to occur (T) anticipate, count on
Prepare: (D) furnish (T) foresee, arrange beforehand
Precaution: (D) care beforehand (T) careful, foresee
Ready: (D) available, to use immediately (T) alert, swift

Page 36   THE STEWARD'S MAZE

1. Lethal Rooms: Bat, Snake Pit, Sharks, Spider, Eyes in Cave

2. Can Represent: Bankruptcy, Poverty, Bad Credit, Disaster, Ignorance, Lust, Drug or Alcohol Addiction

3. Wise Steward – Yes. The route to get in is the same route to get back out

4. Lazy Steward – No. Only found Lethal Rooms

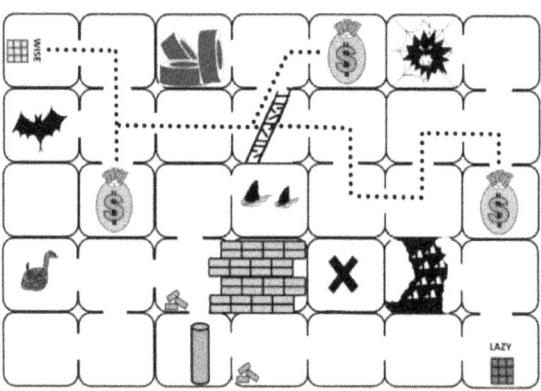

Answer Key Continued

Page 40   <u>FAMILY DEFINITIONS</u>

Furnish:	(D) supply, provide (T) fit, equip
Obligation:	(D) binding contract (T) responsibility, duty
Provide	(D) make available, supply (T) replenish
Provision	(D) provide for the future (T) preparation
Require:	(D) insist, need (T) to want, have need, expect
Responsible:	(D) know right/wrong (T) accountable, stable
Supply:	(D) provide what is needed (T) furnish, fulfill

Page 43   FIX THE STEWARD'S BUDGET - *Suggestions:*

- Pay tithes on the net ($200) until the budget is under control *
- Reduce offerings
- Reduce Savings
- The mortgage remains the same until paid off; pay on time (no late fees)
- Electric bill - wear more clothing in winter; turn off air conditioner and heat when at work
- Plan meals, buy in bulk; take lunch to work
- Keep telephone/cell phone at a minimum
- Keep Cable bill at a minimum
- Buy a transit pass instead of driving a car
- Reduce Charity
- Reduce surplus money; rent movies, potluck/movie night at home; eat at home <u>before</u> going anywhere.

Another option is to tithe 1%, then increase to 2%, etc., until reaching your goal of 10 %

REMEMBER:

There are <u>always</u> options when scheduling or rescheduling your budget

Answer Key Continued

Page 47   SHARING DEFINITIONS
Absolute: (D) perfect, positive, real (T) total, complete
Complete: (D) whole, thorough, absolute (T) not lacking, intact
Free: (D) liberty, (T) self-ruling, unconstrained
Loving: (D) expressing love (T) admiring, respecting, valuing
Perfect: (D), flawless, absolute (T) faultless, unblemished
Unlimited: (D) no restrictions, immeasurable (D) unending
Vast: (D) great in size or degree (T) huge, enormous

Page 49   BUILDING BLOCKS
$2,000 x .02% = $40 divided by 10 = $4 each; or $40 to one charity

Page 53   SURPLUS DEFINITIONS
Adjust: (D) regulate (T) settle, conclude, complete, balance
Balanced: (D) mental or emotional stability (T) surplus, equal
Harmony: (D) agreement in action, ideas (T) compatibility
Peaceful: (D) no disturbance, calm, peace (T) quiet, tranquil
Remainder: (D) what is left of anything (T) surplus, balance
Rest: (D motionless, relief, ease, (T) sleep, slumber, relax
Stability   (D) steadiness (T) durability, endurance, balance

Page 58   IN THE DARK:

One who manages another's property, finances, or other affairs

Answer Key Continued

Page 59   WORD SEARCH

Tithes, Taxes, Offerings, Savings, Family, Sharing, Surplus
Bonus Word: Wise

B	F	A	C	D	E	F	G	S
S	A	V	I	N	G	S	H	T
G	Y	L	I	M	A	F	E	A
N	E	T	A	X	E	S	O	R
I	R	S	U	L	P	R	U	S
R	S	I	O	N	S	O	W	U
E	T	T	N	E	C	R	I	P
F	T	I	T	H	E	S	S	L
F	F	W	L	X	O	T	E	R
O	P	S	H	A	R	I	N	G

Answer Key Continued

Page 60   STEWARD-SHIP-WRECK

Giving First:	Tithes	
Obedience to Authority:	Taxes	
Continuity:	Offerings	
Preparation:	Savings	
Provision:	Family	
Unconditional Love:	Sharing	
Balance:	Surplus	

Page 61   HIDDEN TAX LETTER

Tax, taxes, taxicab, taxidermist, overtaxed, taxable, taxpayer, surtaxes, syntax, taxation, overtaxed

Page 62   UN*SCRAMBLE*

Tithes, Taxes, Offerings, Savings, Family, Share, Surplus

Additional Reading for Parents

Everyone needs to learn the difference between wise and unwise stewardship, and the Bible has many examples. One can discover that stewardship is required both in our natural and spiritual lives.

The first example of unwise stewardship occurred in heaven with the archangel Lucifer. God created him as a steward over the other angels; however, all angels were God's stewards. Foolishly, Lucifer decided that he could overthrow God's throne and authority because his beauty and chief position should make him Heaven's leader rather than God, the one who made him. Lucifer erroneously thought he could coerce all angles to side with him, but only one-third of the angels did, and they suffered immediate humiliation and consequences! *(Isaiah 14:12-14)*

Because Lucifer mismanaged his heavenly stewardship responsibilities, God stripped them from him and kicked Lucifer out of heaven! A third of the angels who sided with Lucifer were also kicked out from their home's comfort in heaven, never to return. *(Hebrews 1:7, Psalms 103:20, Revelations 12:7-9)*

Another example of unwise stewardship was Adam and Eve, the first man and woman God created on the earth. God shared with them His likeness, placed them in the beautiful Garden of Eden as their home, and gave them stewardship instructions. Simply stated, they were to imitate God's dominion on earth, just like God has authority in heaven. How do we know? The Lord's prayer is an example. When the disciples asked Jesus to teach them to pray. Jesus said, *"Thy will be done, as in heaven, so on earth ..." (Luke 11:2)*

Too, while Adam and Eve were to "dress and keep" the garden, it also meant for Adam to care for, guard, and protect it. Yet, Adam allowed a serpent from the wilderness to enter their home and question God's instructions and authority. However, Lucifer, now renamed Satan, was the one to use the serpent for his evil intent.

God had already instructed Adam NOT to eat *the fruit from the tree of good and evil knowledge*, but he and Eve did anyway. *(Genesis 2:16-17)* Even though the serpent tricked Eve into eating it, and God was angry with her, more importantly, God was more enraged with Adam because his disobedience was willful! He was with Eve the entire time during the conversation with the serpent. Adam willfully chose to eat it despite God telling him not to do it. Rather than accept responsibility for his actions, Adam didn't repent or ask for forgiveness but instead blamed God for giving him the woman, then blamed her for giving him the fruit to eat. *(Genesis 3:9-12)*

Unfortunately, in their disobedience to God, Adam and Eve relinquished their dominion and stewardship to Satan, thus causing disobedience and sin in man. *(Genesis 3:22-24)*. God put a curse on them and then forced Adam and Eve to leave the comfort of their home in Eden, and reside in the wilderness, never to return.

God also dealt with the serpent who allowed Satan to use him *(just like Satan did with Judas)*. Since the serpent caused Adam and Eve to be defenseless, God cursed the snake to be defenseless as well by having it crawl on its stomach forever!

There are many examples in the Bible of wise stewardship. One was with Abraham. God said that He knew Abraham would make sure that everyone in his household obeyed God, and He blessed them for it. *(Genesis 18:19)*

Joshua was a successful steward after Moses died. Joshua ensured that God's people entered the promised land. However, Joshua learned the hard way about listening to people rather than listening to God. When Joshua followed God's instructions, he was successful. *(Joshua 1:9)* As soon as he listened to other's opinions, Joshua failed! *(Joshua 5:18-19, 7:1-5)* After Joshua repented, God forgave him and caused him to succeed, prosper, and live the rest of his life in peace.

An example of both wise and unwise financial stewardship in the Bible is the parable of the talents with three servants – two wise and one foolish. A man was going on a trip and gave his servants some of his money to manage while he was away. *(Matthew 25:14-29)* Once home, he asked them for his money. Two servants said that they invested it and doubled his money! It pleased the man very much! In return, he gave them bonuses! The third servant did *nothing* with the money given him to manage, which made the man very angry. He could see that this servant was too lazy and selfish, so he immediately kicked him out of the comfort of his home to fend for himself.

As we recognize that we're all God's Stewards, we will want to imitate God's pattern and principles for successful living. *(Proverbs 1:6-7)* We must be good stewards over it and care about the cleanliness and the atmospheres around us– the sky, air, oceans, lakes, and earth so that future generations will also enjoy the benefits of Creation. It will ensure that they will live, thrive, and survive too. The beauty in Creation is that it's all around us as a reminder of the principles found within it!

Also, we must be good stewards over our spiritual existence, not only in this life but with our eternal life. Everyone will choose where they will spend it - with or without God. Children must understand that this is an individual choice, so no one, not even a parent, can decide for them. They must decide for themselves.

Lastly, one day, everyone will account for their stewardship to God for all given them to love, care and protect during their lifetime, including His purpose for them. God placed it in everyone's heart, and it is up to each one to discover it. Sometimes people sense it in their intuition, talent, and intentionally asking God in prayer. As we mature from children to adults, everyone will make mistakes along the way, but the love of God will always allow us to repent and begin again. Why? Because we are all God's children!

Jesus Christ, the Wisest Steward of all!

Scriptural References – King James Version

Principle One:

Genesis 28:22	*Proverbs 3:9*	*Malachi 3:8, 10*	*I Corinthians 15:23*

Principle Two:

Matthew 6:10	*Matthew 28:18*	*Luke 20:25*	*Romans 13:1,7*

Principle Three:

Exodus 35:5	*Deuteronomy 16:17*	*Hebrews 10:10*	*II Corinthians 9:7*

Principle Four:

Deuteronomy 28:5	*Matthew 25:20*	*Matthew 25:21*	*John 14:2c*

Principle Five:

Psalm 68:6	*Proverbs 22:6*	*Proverbs 31:27-28*	*I Timothy 5:8*

Principle Six:

Genesis 1:26-28	*Matthew 22:39*	*Mark 16:15*	*John 3:16*

Principle Seven:

Psalm 23:2-3a	*Proverbs 10:22*	*John 14:27*	*Hebrews 4:9*

Introduction References: II Corinthians 1:9-12
Preface References: Nehemiah 1-4, and chapter 6

Additional Resources

An Expository Dictionary of Biblical Words, W.E. Vine. Thomas Nelson 1985

The New American Roget's College Thesaurus in Dictionary Form. Grosset & Dunlap 1973

Webster's New World Dictionary and Thesaurus, 2nd Edition. Wiley 2002

About Denise I. Griggs

Denise. Griggs is the Publisher and Owner of Glass Tree Books® and Blue Eclipse Publishing.®

Ms. Griggs has a Master's Degree in Education from a Christian University and is the author of several books for children and young adults. She writes on various topics such as Diversity, Genealogy, and Theology.

Denise is also a genealogist and has researched her maternal ancestors back to the 8th century. She has taught genealogy seminars in the community on researching their family history and techniques to uncover obstacles and barriers in genealogical research. Ms. Griggs has been written about in newspapers, appeared on television, taught theology sermons, and recently finished a genealogy documentary.

Ms. Griggs and her family reside in California, and she loves technology, research, writing, speaking, art, and travel.

Books By Denise I. Griggs

Children

Glass Tree Books®
http://www.glasstreebooks.com

Diversity *(Includes Worksheets)*
 Series: featuring Jan and Denetria
- *The Great Mysterious Adventure*
- *Our Skin Color Is Our Clothing, Field Trip to the Zoo*

Theology
- *The Creation Story: Told by the Wise and Majestic Oak Tree (companion book for The Wise Steward Book, for Children Only!)*

Genealogy
- *I Know Who I Am On the Family Tree, A Children's Genealogy Beginner Guide (Workbook)*

Teens & Young Adults

Blue Eclipse Publishing ®
http://www.blue-eclipse-publishing.com

Genealogy
- *A Mulatto Slave, the Events in the Life of Peter Hunt, 1844-1915 (Includes Topics for Research, Discussion, Worksheets, Historical Timeline, & Pictures)*

Theology
- *Return to the Table, Beware the Presence (A Fictional Christian Thriller)*

www.ingramcontent.com/pod-product-compliance
Lightning Source LLC
Chambersburg PA
CBHW082055090726
47909CB00010B/3042